TIM
ALL ALONE

by

Edward Ardizzone

Henry Z. Walck, Inc.
New York

For my cousin Victoria

First published 1956

STANDARD BOOK NUMBER: 8098-1048-4

LIBRARY OF CONGRESS CATALOG CARD NUMBER: CD 62-229

PRINTED IN THE UNITED STATES OF AMERICA

One day Tim arrived back at his home by the sea. He had been away for a long holiday and was therefore longing to see his mother and father again.

Imagine, however, his surprise when he found the windows shuttered and the door locked.

He looked through the keyhole and found nobody.

He shouted but no one answered.

Then he noticed a
bit of paper pinned
beside the door. It
said 'Gone away.
House to Let'.

Poor Tim. He sat
down on the step and
wondered and
wondered what
strange thing could
have happened.

However, when
he had cried a little –
and he could not help
that – he remembered
to say his prayers and
felt a little comforted.

Then he got up, turned his back on the house and set out on his way once more.

He was determined to search, if necessary, the whole wide world until he had found his parents.

But Tim had no money, so he stopped at a farm-house and asked the farmer to give him a bed for the night.

'You can sleep in my hay loft,' said the

farmer, 'and I will give you breakfast and dinner too, but first you must dig my potato patch.' He gave Tim a fork and set him to work.

When night came and Tim lay down in the hay, he felt too tired to be sad, but went straight to sleep.

At breakfast the next morning Tim told his story.

The good farmer's wife felt sorry for him, so when he came to leave she gave him a large packet of sandwiches and two very rosy apples, slipped some money in his pocket and kissed him goodbye.

Tim's plan was to join one of the small ships which stopped at all the little ports up and down the coast where he could inquire for his parents. He knew they loved the sea and would not live far away from it.

So Tim marched to the seaport town and here his luck was good, for lying in the dock was the very ship he wanted. A little old ship with a tall red funnel, called the *Amelia Jane*. Luckier still, when Tim went on board,

he found they were short of crew and he was
signed on at once as a cabin boy.

Once at sea Tim was kept so busy painting,
scrubbing, running errands and helping the
steward serve the officers' meals that he had
little time to fret.

The *Amelia Jane* was a happy ship and all the officers and crew were kindly men and particularly kind to Tim.

The days and weeks went by and at every little port at which they stopped, and there were many of them, Tim would hurry ashore

and inquire for his father and mother.

How unhappy he felt when he heard no news of them and how sadly he went back to join his ship.

It was then that the officers and crew were specially nice to him and tried their best to cheer him up.

But perhaps Tim's best friend on board was the ship's cat.

Many a time when work was done Tim would sit in some sheltered corner of the deck and talk to the cat and tell him his life's story.

The cat would answer 'Prrmp, prrmp, miaou, miaou,' as if he understood every word of it.

Now don't forget this cat because, later

on, he is going to play a very important part in this tale.

One day the *Amelia Jane* was docked in a small port and Tim, as usual, had been on shore looking for his parents.

He was hurrying back to the ship, having

searched in vain, when he saw a lady stand-
ing on the pavement. He stopped and, as a
last chance, asked her if she knew of them.
'What! lost your parents, have you?' said

the lady catching hold of Tim by the hand.
'Then you must come with me to the home
for lost children!'
'No, no,' said Tim, 'I don't want to go to

a home for lost children; I'm a sailor and must get to my ship now, or I will miss it. Please do let go.'

But the lady held on to his hand as tightly as ever and dragged him along the streets

till they came to a great dark house with a great dark door.

'Here we are,' she said, taking out a big key and trying to fit it into the keyhole.

At that moment Tim gave a sharp tug which made her drop the key. Then, when

she bent down to pick it up, he tugged again and she fell over and let go his hand.

Away went Tim, running as fast as he could, back towards the docks.

But you can imagine his dismay, for when he arrived at the quayside he saw the *Amelia Jane* steaming out to sea. He had missed his ship.

There was only one thing for Tim to do, he must hide. So he slipped on board another steamer and hid under one of the boats.

It was not long before he heard the engines being started and the sound of ropes being

let go and he was out at sea once more.

But this new ship was not a happy one like the old *Amelia Jane*. The captain was a horrid man and the crew were a rough and unfriendly lot. They were all particularly horrid to Tim because he was a stowaway.

The weather was bad, yet every day Tim was made to work on deck. He was frozen by the cold North wind and often soaked with rain or salt sea spray.

After a time Tim felt sick, too sick to work.

The captain was furious. 'I can't have sick boys on board,' he shouted. 'Send him ashore.'

The ship was hove-to near a small grey seaside town and a signal was sent for a boat to come to the ship.

When it was alongside, Tim was lowered

into the boat and away it went.

Arriving at the town Tim was landed on the stone

jetty of the little harbour.

Among the people watching him being lifted

out of the boat was a middle-aged lady who took pity on him.

'Ah! the poor wee lad,' she said. 'Carry him to my house and I will nurse him and look after him.' So the boatman carried him up to a small grey house on the hill behind the town, where he was put to bed.

Here he lay sick for many days and Miss Hetty McBain, for that was the lady's name, was very kind to him and nursed him very well.

She gave him porridge and cream, good rich milk and new laid eggs.

Gradually Tim became better, and one
day when he was nearly well Miss Hetty
said, 'Tim, my boy, I have a plan. I am get-
ting old now and lonely. Stay with me and
be my son.'

Tim asked if he could first go away and look for his parents, but Miss Hetty would not hear of it. This made Tim sad because he loved Miss Hetty and did not want to hurt her feelings.

Every day, when Tim was allowed out, he would walk down to the little harbour

and stare out to sea and long so much to be away, and every day he became sadder and sadder.

One morning at breakfast Miss Hetty said, 'Tim, my boy, how sad you look. I see now that I must let you go.' Then she gave him a suitcase full of new clothes and

some money and kissed him goodbye.

Tim set off feeling both happy and sorry too. But when he reached the harbour he saw something that made him feel really happy, for lying by the jetty was the old *Amelia Jane*.

What a welcome he had on board! How pleased they all were to see him! And the ship's cat was the most pleased of all.

Of course the captain insisted that he should be their cabin boy again.

But Tim's troubles were not over yet.
They had not been at sea many days when
they ran into bad weather, and, worse still,
the ship caught fire.

Tim smelt the smoke first and rushed to
tell the captain.

Alas, the strong wind fanned the flames

and though the crew worked like heroes they could not put the fire out. At last all the forward part of the ship was ablaze.

Sadly the captain gave the order to abandon ship and they clambered into the remaining boats.

At that moment Tim remembered the cat
which had been shut up in the mate's cabin.

'Oh, poor cat! I must save it,' he cried,
and dashed back on deck, though the crew
tried to stop him.

He reached the cabin and caught the cat,

but when he turned to go back he found
that the flames had leapt up behind him
and he could not return.

All that Tim could do was to plunge
into the sea with the cat in his arms.

Luckily Tim saw a hatch cover floating

nearby which the crew had thrown over-
board earlier. He and the cat climbed on
to it.

Now the waves were too high and the
spray too thick for the crews of the boats
to find them, so all that day Tim and the
cat drifted across the stormy sea.

At dusk they were cast up on a sandy
beach.

They climbed the steep beach and found
themselves in the streets of a seaside town.

They stopped at a café and peered through the lighted windows. They were both cold, wet, tired and very very hungry. But Tim had no money to buy any food.

Then Tim noticed through the glass a

lady sitting all by herself at a table. She was holding a handkerchief to her eyes as if she was crying.

COULD IT BE HIS MOTHER?

Yes it was.

In a moment Tim was in the café and in his mother's arms.

How happy they were and what a lot they had to tell each other!

Tim's mother explained that when he was on holiday, they read in a newspaper that a pleasure steamer had been lost at sea with all on board. By some terrible mistake Tim's name was given as one of the passengers. They were so sad that they could not bear to live any longer in the old house and so had decided to go away.

Tim told her all about his adventures.

The next day Tim and his parents and the
ship's cat all went back to the old home by
the sea.

They found it was still un-Let and just
the same as before.

Tim's friends Charlotte and Ginger came
back to stay with them and they all lived
happily there ever afterwards

BUT

You may be sure Tim did not forget Miss Hetty.

Nor did he forget his good friends on the *Amelia Jane*, who had all landed safely.

THE END